To the Robins of today and tomorrow.

This project was published by The Friends of Rutherford House Society.
11153 Saskatchewan Dr NW, Edmonton, AB T6G 2S1

Hardcover Edition ISBN: 978-0-9948434-2-5

Written, illustrated and designed locally in Edmonton, Alberta.
Printed and bound in Canada.
The illustrations were created with india ink and assembled/coloured digitally.

FSC
www.fsc.org
FSC® C016245
MIX
Paper from
responsible sources

Robin ran up the steps of the old brick house on Saskatchewan Drive. "Come on, Grandma!" she shouted from the top. "Coming, dear," Grandma said. "I smell cookies!" Robin said. "They have cookies here?" "They do," Grandma said. "And tea."

Robin followed the smell of cookies into the kitchen. The cookies were in the oven but they weren't ready yet. "Grandma, that oven looks funny," Robin said.

"It's a very old oven," Grandma said.

SNIFF

"Older than my big brother?" Robin asked. "Much older," Grandma said. "It's almost as old as Edmonton, I imagine."

"Grandma, cities don't have ages," Robin said. "They certainly do," Grandma said. "Lots of things happened here even before I was born." "What things?" Robin asked.

Rutherford looked disappointed. "I think I'll go for a walk," he said.

"Rutherford is a time-travelling moose," Grandma said.

"He can show you what Edmonton was like a long time ago."

"And bring you back in time for those cookies," Rutherford said.

"Let's go!" Robin said.

Robin climbed on Rutherford's back.
"Hang on tight," he said. "Here we go!"
Suddenly, the old brick house was gone.
The whole city was gone.
Now there was nothing but ice and snow.

Where's Edmonton?

"This is the Looooong Ago," Rutherford
explained. "There's no Edmonton yet.
Not a lot happens here. But I kind of like it.

Most of the ice had melted now. Grass was growing and birds were singing.
Robin saw a ring of teepees with people outside them.

"There are kids playing!" Robin said.
"The First People live here now," Rutherford said.
"It's a good place to meet and to hunt."

Some kids ran along the riverbank with their dog.
They smiled and waved at Robin.

Some people in long canoes came paddling up the river.

"Who are they?" Robin asked.

"Explorers and traders started coming here in the Looong Ago," Rutherford said. "They're bringing things to trade for furs with the people who live here."

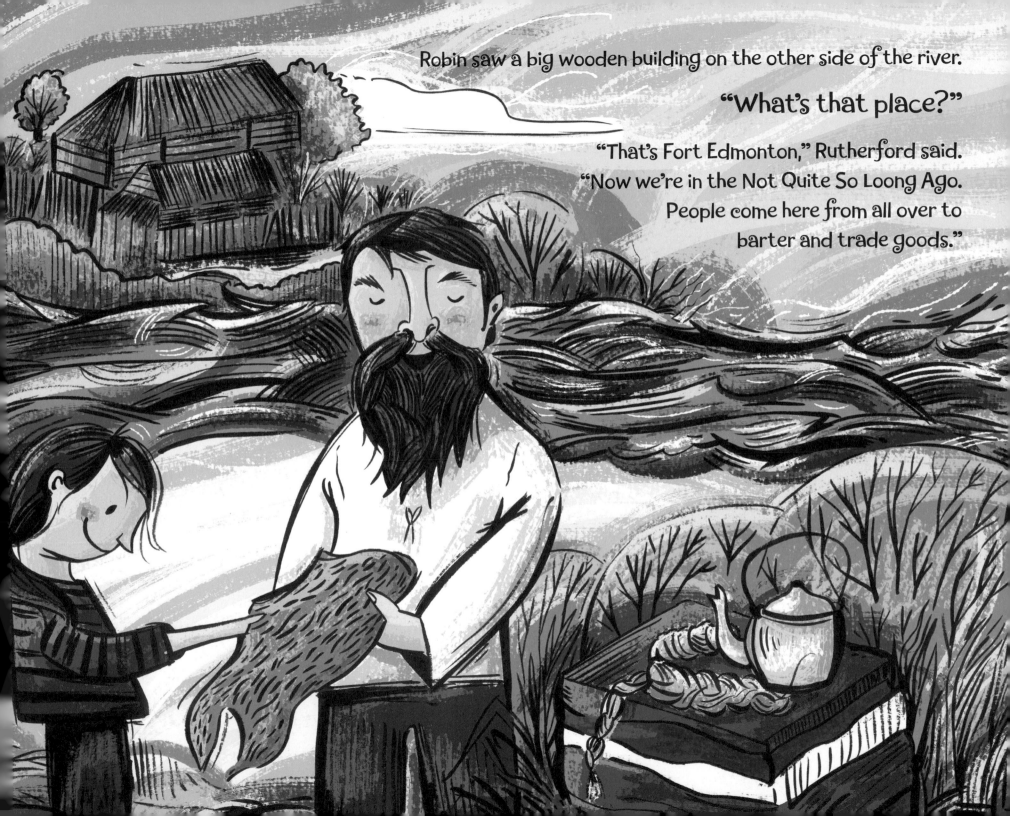

Robin saw a big wooden building on the other side of the river.

"What's that place?"

"That's Fort Edmonton," Rutherford said. "Now we're in the Not Quite So Loong Ago. People come here from all over to barter and trade goods."

"Let's go to the fort!" Robin said.

"We have to take the ferry across the river because there's no bridge yet," Rutherford said.
"My friend John Walter is a busy man, but I bet he can help us."

John Walter was standing at the ferry crossing, checking his pocketwatch.

"You're just in time, Rutherford," John Walter said. "I'm about to head across."

John Walter took Robin and Rutherford across the river on the ferry.

The river was very wide and flowed very fast. Robin held on to Rutherford's antlers.

When they got to the other side, Robin was surprised.
Fort Edmonton was gone. Where the fort had been stood
a large stone building with a big dome on top.

"I've seen that place before," Robin said.

"That's the Legislature," Rutherford said.
"It's still there where you come from. I mean,
WHEN you come from."

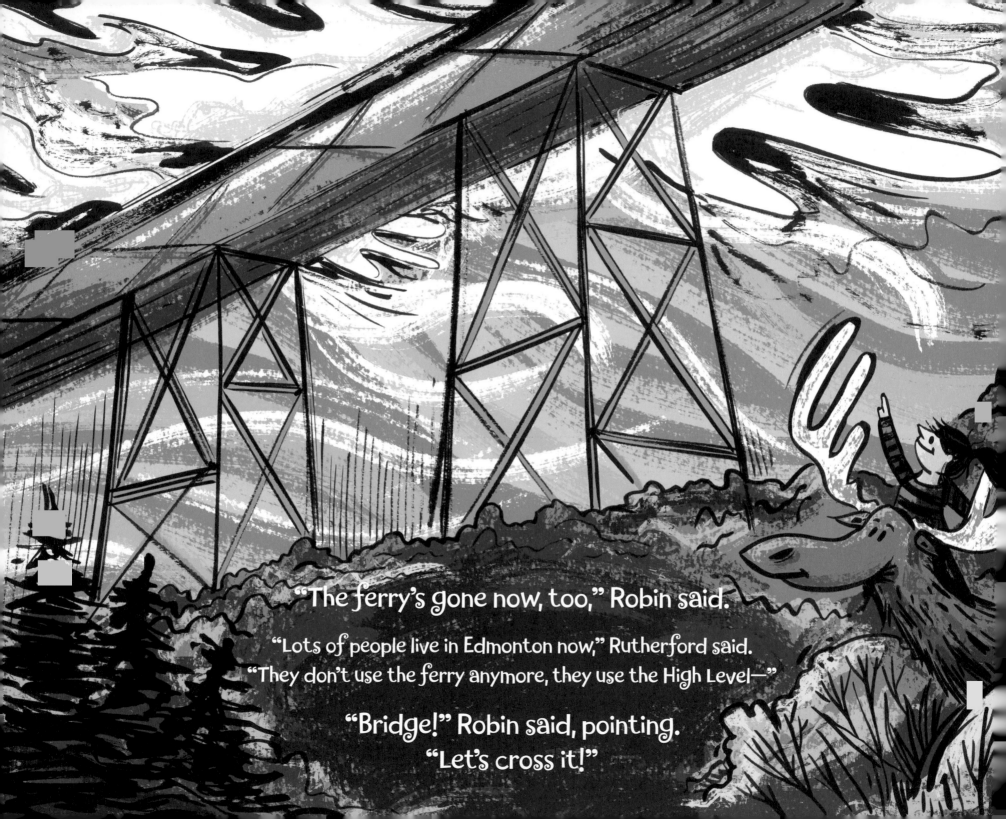

"The ferry's gone now, too," Robin said.

"Lots of people live in Edmonton now," Rutherford said.
"They don't use the ferry anymore, they use the High Level—"

"Bridge!" Robin said, pointing.
"Let's cross it!"

The streetcar crossed the river way up high on the bridge.

It was a long way down to the water.

The streetcar took them to the train station. Families were climbing off the train with their luggage and trunks.

"Edmonton is a boom town now," Rutherford said. "Folks are coming to live here from all over the world."

Rutherford trotted past the red brick library.

"I've been there with my Grandma," Robin said.

"This is the Not All That Long Ago. We're almost back when we came from."

Rutherford walked up the avenue.

Robin saw more streetcars, and buses
going up and down, and people
hurrying along with shopping bags.

Everybody smiled and waved.
Robin waved back.

Robin looked around. "Where did the streetcars go?" she asked.

"There are more cars and buses now," Rutherford said.
"Too many for the streetcars to fit on the roads."

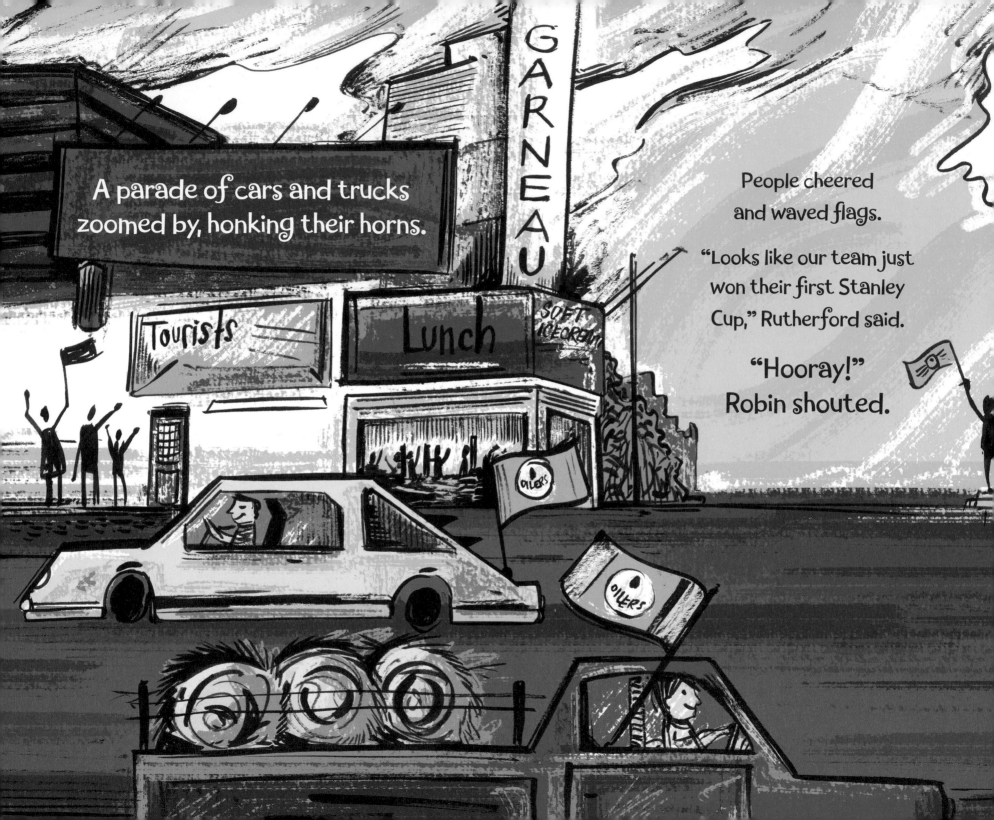

A parade of cars and trucks zoomed by, honking their horns.

People cheered and waved flags.

"Looks like our team just won their first Stanley Cup," Rutherford said.

"Hooray!" Robin shouted.

Robin saw the old brick house.

"That's where we came from!" Robin said. "I mean, WHEN we came from."

"I sure hope those cookies are ready," Rutherford said.

Grandma was waiting for them in the kitchen, and the cookies WERE ready.

And there was a surprise ...

EVERYBODY was there. It was a party!

When the party was over, everyone went back to WHEN they belonged.

Rutherford had to go, too.

"When do YOU come from, Rutherford?" Robin asked.

"From now and then," Rutherford said. "A lot of things from long ago are still here, if you know where to look."

"History is all around us," Grandma said.
"History is what my brother learns in school," Robin said.
"It's also what we make, every day," Grandma said.
"Each one of us."

THE END

FRIENDS *of* RUTHERFORD HOUSE SOCIETY

EDMONTON
HERITAGE COUNCIL

THE CITY OF
Edmonton